JAUNTS WITH JACK

Gavin R Dobson

Other books by the author:

Geordie Kinloch Short stories:
Tales of a Free Spirit – ISBN 1-904440-66-5
The Novice – ISBN 1-904440-95-9
Side Trips – ISBN 978-1-906775-09-4
The Global Investor, Probus/McGraw Hill 1994 – ISBN 1 55738 556 4

Novel: The Price of Redemption – ISBN 978-1-906775-28-5

Published by the author

ISBN 978-0-9575835-0-4

Copies can be ordered from retail or from:

Gavin R Dobson
Logie House
Kirriemuir
DD8 5PN

Printed in Castellar 20pt /Calibri 12pt

Text layout by Robertson Printers, Forfar

Cover design by Gavin Dobson and Robertson Printers, Forfar

Printed and bound in Great Britain by Robertson Printers, Forfar

DEDICATION

This little book is dedicated to the staff of Balhousie Nursing Home in Coupar Angus for their hard work, patience and never-ending good humour.

CONTENTS

PREFACE

Jaunts with Jack is an account of the life-long friendship between a boy and his aunt. It opens in the innocence of prep school life in Sussex in the 1950s and closes in the innocence of japes in the Angus Glens fifty years later.

Joan Ritchie was a Scottish orthodontist who established her practice in Cavendish Square in London in the 1950s. She worked very hard and lived a stylish life, drawing her friends and patients from many countries around the world. Two traits they all shared with Jack were a considerable sense of fun and a staunch loyalty for each other.

When I was a schoolboy in Sussex she used to drive down from London in her shiny green Wolseley on exit Sundays. If the weather was fine she brought a picnic hamper. If it was wet, she took us to the Mermaid in Rye or the Star in Alfriston. Whatever the weather, lunch was always followed by a brisk walk along the beach or useful activities like jumping into her car to see how far it would freewheel with the engine off. Every outing ended with cakes and cocoa before she bundled us back to school in time for evensong.

The middle years were busy times. Jack's practice became world-renowned as she straightened the teeth of the rich and famous. She never told us their names, bound as she was by the dental equivalent of the Official Secrets Act. But signed photographs of smiling stars in her kitchen were a giveaway: without compromising her they provided her nephew with considerable bragging rights.

I worked overseas for many years; we kept in touch over holidays and birthdays. I called her when I stopped over in the UK; we met in London or, increasingly, at her cottage in the deliciously-named Steeple Bumpstead.

In her seventies, she developed a relationship with an old friend; he was a widower and retired dental surgeon called Alan Campbell. For ten years they travelled together, entertained at their respective homes, laughed a great deal and loved each other's company. Alan was one of nature's gentlemen, a perfect match for Jack.

Life's circles brought us closer as time went on. My mother—Jack's older sister Dorothy—died in April 2008. After the funeral, with appropriate humour, Jack donned the mantle of Family Matriarch. When my father died unexpectedly a month later; Jack was all there, one hundred per cent, a tower of strength. To my regret I was so consumed with my parents at this time that I failed to appreciate that dear Alan was fading. He died in the summer of 2008 with Jack by his side.

It was time to make decisions. Jack spent Christmas 2008 with us on the farm in Scotland. She missed Alan and, at the age of 85, was beginning to find the administration of her affairs quite onerous. After we discussed the possibility of taking over an empty cottage on the farm, she perked up. We all agreed that it would be good for her to move to Scotland, back to the bosom of her family. This was followed by numerous site visits, changes of plan and the interminable sorting of STUFF.

She closed the door of her cottage in Steeple Bumpstead for the last time in the Autumn of 2009. I bundled her into a white Ford Transit and we headed north. A whole new chapter of jaunts with Jack had begun.

In writing this little book I hope I don't imply that I have any sort of monopoly of Jack's affections among family and friends. Everyone who has been close to her has special anecdotes. I was fortunate as a young boy that she was able to spend so many free weekends with me. In her old age I've been privileged to spend similar amounts of time with her, thus repaying, in very small measure, the days of family fun we had such a long time ago.

EARLY DAYS

Joan Garrick Ritchie was born in a holiday house in Dunbar at 4pm on Monday July 9th 1923. I can picture the summer breeze from the North Sea and the billowing lace curtains as Joan was laid in her mother Winifred's arms. At that moment Winifred announced that something wasn't quite right. She handed the newborn baby to her sister Gladys, who was helping with the *accouchement*, and promptly delivered a beautiful twin daughter. Gladys looked up and asked, "Is that all now, Winifred?" to which the exhausted mother replied, "I hope so."

It is hard to imagine this scene today, but that is how it happened on July 9th 1923.

There were already three sisters in the Ritchie family: Win, Dorothy and Anne. Together they decided that the twins were to be named Gertrude and Daisy in honour of two cows grazing in a nearby pasture. After a great deal of argy bargy with the grown-ups the twins were named Joan and Jill, on condition that Joan would always be named Jack.

Win announced that she would take special responsibility for Jill, and Dorothy would be in charge of baby Jack. Anne, by all accounts the cleverest child in the family, seems to have been above such nonsense. In the fullness of time Dorothy would also be my mother.

The family lived in Dollar, near Stirling. Over the next 18

years, each girl was to pass through Dollar Academy with distinction. As the school historian has observed, there were few honours or positions that at least one Ritchie girl did not attain: The Milne Prize, Dux (Head Girl), Physics medal, French medal, German medal, Hockey team and so forth. There was a gap in the music area, but I suspect that music was not a priority in our Presbyterian Granny's solo upbringing of five girls. My grandfather was in the Indian Civil Service and had generously delegated the entire raising of his family to his wife in Scotland.

From the mid-1920s to the late 1930s summer holidays consisted of epic camping trips to St Cyrus Bay in Kincardineshire. The coal merchant in Dollar would scrub out his truck, load it with tents, sleeping bags, camp beds, trestle tables, folding chairs, stores, rolls of canvas and all the paraphernalia essential to five young girls and their friends.

My grandmother travelled with the coal merchant in the cab; all the girls, their friends and two dogs—Nippy and Ray—piled into the rear of the truck and huddled under the tarpaulin for the eighty mile drive from Dollar to St Cyrus. They amused themselves by sticking their tongues out at passing strangers from the back. This was, mercifully, long before the stupefying hand of Health and Safety ruined everyone's fun.

On arrival the first task of the coal merchant was to dig a latrine, build a frame and erect a canvas screen around it. Then the high circular canvas tents went up. The girls helped carry provisions down the cliff path and got the site arranged. Then my grandmother organized tea and sandwiches, confirmed his return date in August and waved goodbye to the coal merchant. The Ritchie girls were consigned to the sand dunes of St Cyrus for the summer. And they loved it.

St Cyrus was to provide some of the happiest days of their lives. I grew up with tales of endless sunny days, excited girls splashing in the chilly water, fishing for crabs, flying kites, dogs going mad in the surf, meticulously-sliced triangular sandwiches, bicycle expeditions into the Kincardineshire hinterland, hikes to explore Dunottar Castle, curious boys venturing down to the beach from neighbouring farms, stories around the campfire. And no doubt, periodic sulks as the girls grew pubescent.

SCHOOL DAYS

Jack flourished at Dollar Academy. She was Head Girl in 1940 under the redoubtable Rector Harry Bell. She won the Physics and French medals and played in the Hockey team. Her fine intellect tended towards the sciences, so she went to Queen's College, St Andrews University to study dentistry. Queen's College was in Dundee, where she took rooms with a family in 22 Windsor Street for the duration of her studies.

History doesn't relate what she got up to at university, but her mother Winifred used to stay in her lodgings for long stretches of time. This doesn't seem to have bothered Jack in the slightest. One assumes that she was too busy studying to worry about her style being cramped, unlike most students today. I can't believe that she wasn't pursued by admirers, however. By the age of 19 Jack had grown into a stunning young woman with flowing locks of wavy auburn hair.

On the 26th June 1945 she was awarded her Licentiateship in Dental Surgery from St Andrews University. This was followed five years later by a Diploma in Dental Orthopaedics from the Royal Faculty of Physicians and Surgeons of Glasgow. Jack was the only female DDO RFPS (Glasgow) graduate in 1950.

THE YOUNG PROFESSIONAL

Jack moved to London in 1951, having been offered an internship at a dental practice in 19 Harcourt House, 19 Cavendish Square. Shortly afterwards the senior partner retired for health reasons and offered Jack his practice. At the tender age of 28, she established what was to become one of the premier orthodontic practices in Great Britain.

Her premises were on the first floor of a handsome Regency town house. At street level it boasted a grand portico, a secure entrance hall, a cockney doorman, a creaky lift and wide stairs. The building smelled of brass polish and antique furniture wax. It was one of the grandest professional addresses in London, just a block from Harley Street.

The public part of Jack's floor consisted of a hall, two large practice rooms facing the square, an office and a waiting room. The calming aura of an exotic fish aquarium greeted patients in the waiting room. An internal stair led down to the dental technician's workshop, filled, as I recall, with dusty boxes of children's dental moulds from floor to ceiling.

Another flight of steps led up to the private mezzanine where Jack lived. It consisted of two bedrooms, an elegant drawing room, a kitchen and a bathroom dominated by a splendid cast iron bath with a long heavy stopper. Her flat was decorated with style and business-like femininity. There was nothing pink and fluffy about it; every object was meticulously-placed for the most striking effect. Her kitchen was the *dernier cri*; it boasted a breakfast counter with bar stools. The surfaces were made of easily-wiped, scratch-free, fireproof laminates; she had a self-lighting oven.

Heaven knows what the cost of such an arrangement would be today. It is striking to think how Jack took responsibility for thousands of square feet of overhead in Central London, a secretary, an administrative assistant and a dental technician, all before she'd fully established her own practice.

I'm not sure when I first met Jack. No doubt I was paraded before my aunts as a baby, but my first true memory is at age 8, when my father took me to Harcourt House to be wired up as my new teeth were growing in. I was rigid with fear, but the moment I was presented to the tall, elegant, confidently-smiling lady in a white surgeon's jacket, I knew all would be well.

Jack sat me down in the dentist's chair and asked if I preferred Strawberry or Chocolate. I can't remember the answer but my mouth was soon stuffed with glutinous goop that tasted of neither. I was told to bite hard to leave an imprint, which I did. This led to a plaster cast of my teeth, followed by a two year course of treatment to straighten them.

I had just started at Vinehall, a boys' prep school near Battle in Sussex. My parents had divorced; both lived abroad. Just to head off the toff-bashers, I'll say it now: to this day, I still get rattled when a child whose parents are divorced is regarded as "privileged" when sent away to boarding school.

My brother Alastair was three years older than I. We got on

well and did a lot together, but three years at that age is like belonging to a different planet. He tolerated my juvenile friends but understandably preferred spending time in the company of his own pals. Alastair must have been there, but oddly, my memories are of the times when Jack, often accompanied by Jill, took me out with friends of my own age.

Jack made the offer to come to Sussex and take us out at weekends. She'd just purchased a smart new Forest Green Wolseley 1500 with cream Connolly leather seats and walnut trimmings. How could we resist?

EARLY JAUNTS

I caught Geoffrey's eye as the school thundered into the last verse of the hymn:

Breathe through the heats of our desire,
Thy coolness and thy balm.
Let sense be dumb, let flesh retire

He grinned and cocked his thumb. Any suggestion of flesh to the mind of a ten year old was an opportunity to be, well, precocious. I grinned back knowingly.

Speak through the earthquake, wind and fire,
Oh still small voice of calm

Before the echo of ninety singing—oh all right, shouting--prep school boys had completely died down, the headmaster closed his eyes and raised his right hand:

"To the glory of the Father, the Son and the Holy Ghost, we stand in witness of Thy everlasting bounty and joy and strength. We beseech Thee to watch over all your lambs on this exit Sunday. Amen."

"Amen."

It was eleven o'clock exactly.

"All right boys, you're free to go now. Remember to be back in time for chapel this evening at 6 o'clock." This was followed by a collective screech of joy and the mass-scraping of tubular chairs on Victorian parquet. Ninety overexcited hooligans made for the exit and stampeded along the corridor to the hall where their parents waited.

"AND DON'T RUN IN THE CORRIDORS!" The dear old chap shouted as the last boy disappeared around the corner, adding *sotto voce* "Some bloody lambs."

I raced past Richard's dad, DSO, DFC and two bars for heroic sorties to Narvik and exploits in the Battle of Britain. His kind blue eyes were fortified by a splendid moustache. No, I wasn't going out with him in the MG that day, but he gave me a hearty thump on the shoulder as I ran by. And there was Nick's Mum, a farmer's wife from Goudhurst. She'd bought the first Morris 1000 wooden-framed shooting brake ever seen in Kent. I'd already been in it for an outing two weeks earlier, happily crammed in the back with two Labradors. She had a worried look as I skidded past. She was all Hardy Amies and Chanel. Quite sexy, if I remember.

I shouted to Geoffrey, "Seen Jack?"

"Nope."

Running against the parental tide we burst through the heavy doors onto the gravel drive. After a cursory look in both directions, Geoffrey shouted:

"There she is!"

The Wolseley was reversing into a slot between two Jags. We ran down the drive to meet her. I pulled open her door just as she was setting the handbrake.

"You're late!" I shouted.

It was three minutes past eleven exactly.

"Traffic was bad around Beckenham."

Before Jack had had a chance to leave the car and stretch her legs, we'd clambered in. I was in the front seat with her crocodile handbag and cigarettes, my friend Geoffrey in the rear with her raincoat.

"All right, you monkeys. We're going to Rye for lunch."

She reached into the glove compartment in the walnut fascia, extracted a paper bag and gave it to me. "Here, this'll keep you going until we get there."

"Thanks Auntie Jack. Would you like one?" I peered into the sticky bag of lemon sherbets.

"No thank you; they're for the two of you."

Geoffrey and I sucked the bitter sweets, staring at the hedgerows as the immaculate Wolseley pottered along the Sussex lanes towards Rye. The November rain swept across Romney Marsh. We gazed as the windscreen wipers glided back and forth, but it was not too wet; it was never too wet for Auntie Jack.

“What have you both been up to since I last saw you?”

“Oh, rugger. We beat Boarzell last Saturday and Marlborough House yesterday.”

“Very good. Were you playing?”

“Geoffrey and I are both in the Seconds. We won in the Seconds and the Firsts.”

“Everyone in Sussex must tremble at the thought of playing Vinehall.”

“Except for Seafield. They beat us on Wednesday.”

“And St Ronans.” Geoffrey added helpfully, “They always beat us.”

I often took Geoffrey when I went out with Jack. His father worked in the oil business in Nigeria, his mother was busy producing babies and there was nobody left to take Geoffrey out on weekends. There were six or seven boys like that. The school made sure they were covered. I liked Geoffrey so he always came with me. Jack liked him too, because it meant I always had someone to race up and down the sand dunes with at Camber, or get lost in the woods, or generally rag about and get exhausted with.

“Would you be a darling and reach into my handbag for a

Du Maurier?" Jack switched to more urgent things.

I opened the stylish square orange box and peeled back the silver foil to reveal two rows of sweet smelling Virginias.

"Can I light it for you?"

"Of course."

In a practiced gesture I flipped back the lid of her exquisite lighter with my thumb and flicked its little brass wheel. The flint sparked and a blue gas jet flashed momentarily as I drew on the cigarette. A wisp of blue smoke curled around my face and I handed the fag to Jack.

"Yuk. I don't know how you can do this."

"It's a horrible habit. Don't start."

"I won't".

And I didn't. Despite knowing how to operate the paraphernalia with considerable style, so I reckoned, I was lucky never to be drawn into smoking. I fondled the lighter. It was absolutely the most beautiful object I had ever held in my hand. It was heavy, two inches long, 18k gold with lapis lazuli panels set into the sides. It had been given to her by an admirer. She had many admirers in those days. I know: I was one of them.

"Can I have this when you die, Auntie Jack?"

"Of course." She laughed as I ran my finger over the gold-engraved word *Cartier* on the base of the lighter.

"But not a minute before."

Even though we'd only walked a few hundred yards from the parked car it was nice to get out of the sharp wind that smacked into Rye from the Channel. The Mermaid was a half-timbered, medieval coaching inn. I recall the low ceilings, the open fireplace, the lights sparkling off the glasses and the silverware in the dining room. I close my eyes and hear the murmur of conversation, the tweedy grandparents, the well-behaved prep-school children munching through lamb, the purposeful clink of cutlery, the roast potatoes and mint sauce. My memory is blanketed with the warm congeniality, the smoky haze and the sherry scents of this ancient English inn on a Sunday lunchtime.

Jack didn't blink when Geoffrey and I ordered half pints of cider. She sipped a Gordon's and Tonic followed by a small bottle of claret with her roast beef. We became restless between courses, so Jack sent us into the street to run around the block. We returned, red- cheeked, to plates of trifle and topped-up cider glasses. After lunch we ducked and weaved and staggered and laughed around the cobbled streets and back alley souvenir shops of Rye. Jack showed us the leaded windowpane on which Queen Elizabeth the First was said to have scratched her signature with a diamond. But my eyes were out of focus; I was tipsy for the first time.

Jack bundled us, giggling, into the Wolseley and drove to

the sea. On arrival at Camber Sands, she fixed a silk scarf around her hair, lit a Du Maurier and shooed us out of the car. Geoffrey and I raced over the dunes and sprinted, flat out, to the distant shore line. The tide was a long way out. Rain was speckling out of the sky and the wind was cold, but we took off our shoes and socks and turned cartwheels on the wet sand. Jack was a distant dot sitting on a dune, sheltering from the wind, wrapped in her Aqua Scutum, her thick auburn hair flying around the edge of the scarf like a Bronte heroine's.

At four o'clock, after hours of splashing about, Jack waved at us. We ran back across the beach, puffed over the dunes and collapsed into the car. I never gave a moment's thought to the sand and dirt we dragged into her pristine car. Not once did Jack scold us for being late, for being dirty, for making noise, for anything. And we must have been pretty obnoxious sometimes. All boys are.

The routine was precision-timed. The last port of call of every Sunday outing was the Yew Tree Inn at Catfield. It was run by an ancient retired army chap and his wife, well into their forties. At a quarter to five we'd walk up the garden path, through the yew archway into the low-ceilinged tea shop. Every oak table was crammed with prep school boys and their custodians, counting down the minutes to the 6 o'clock evening service, which meant leaving the Yew Tree at five-forty or five-fifty depending on which prep school you were from. The old army chap knew the score and found a place for everyone, squeezing a heterogeneous mess of school-boys together wherever they would fit.

The first question to the grown-ups as they sat down was, "India, Ceylon, Lapsang Souchong or Earl Grey?" The boys had a choice of hot cocoa, milk or orange juice. Tea was served in Royal Worcester, cocoa in mugs. The real excitement took place at the sideboard, stacked with glutinous cakes. No sooner were we given our seats, than we sprang up again to ogle the selection. As I recall we could take as much cake as would fit on a smallish plate. That usually meant two large slices. A penetrating glare from one's guardian kept the process under control. In those days, hard to believe, we were brought up to be restrained and good-mannered and would have been mortified to be considered greedy.

A lifetime later I still have a clear picture of the Yew Tree's lemon cream sponge, its coffee gateau with icing oozing off the edge, the pecan pie, Battenberg sponge with extra-thick marzipan, trifle oozing with rum, cream on chocolate, cream on custard, cream on apple pie, cream on cream. The Yew Tree's cakes have never been surpassed in a lifetime of gastronomy.

As we departed from the tea shop, the old soldier handed each schoolboy a gold coin with a wink and the endlessly-repeated exhortation to spend it wisely. As soon as we'd clambered into Jack's car, we flipped off the gold covers and munched the chocolate.

Jack always got us back to Vinehall by five-fifty-five. It was part of the thrill. She would laugh as I gave her a sticky kiss, slammed the car door and raced inside. In my memory it was always raining as we ran into the main building. Then we had just enough time to pee and race to Assembly, line up by House and take roll-call. I was in Rushton, Geoffrey was in Saxton.

Sunday evening services were always a bummer. They defined the end of the weekend; I cannot listen to Christian evening liturgy to this day without feeling sad or developing a headache. *Nunc dimittis servum tuum* ... I wonder how Jack's doing on the road back to London ... *Domine secundum* ... in the rain. Blimey, that chocolate cake was ex—kwi--zit ! ...*verbum tuum in pace*.

I always had a headache those evenings. I was too young to understand, but I had already become a lifelong migraine sufferer. The headaches were almost certainly triggered by chocolate, but they remain mixed in my memory with the sorrow of parting from Jack and the boring intonations of Nunc Dimittis.

Another of Jack's favourite destinations was the Star at Alfriston. We'd arrive about 12 noon, scoff an enormous lunch of roast beef, apple pie and ice cream, then, mildly intoxicated, go for an energetic walk on the Downs. It was always raining, as recorded above, and Jack would set up a little regatta of objects to float down the gutter in the road beside the Star. A walnut shell, a toothpick and a fragment of paper napkin would be hastily crafted. The owner of the first mini galleon to reach the grill and tip into the Bottomless Pit of the sewer would win a bag of sherbet lemons.

I was thoroughly spoiled and look back on those prep-school outings through a golden prism of fun. Jill often came down to Sussex with her. While Jack was reputedly the best orthodontist of her generation, her twin sister Jill worked at the BBC in Bush House. She was one of the first women to earn a degree in electrical engineering. That may sound butch, but she was drop-dead gorgeous. The twins looked, and to an 11 year old, they were, identical. But of course no two people are the same and when I was much older I realised that Jack and Jill had quite different temperaments.

After lunch and the walnut regatta we'd go for a squelch in the hills. We'd always put our wellies in the car and slip them on at the first opportunity after lunch. One favourite game required finding a quiet stretch of road in the Downs. Jack would drive to the top of a rise and turn off the ignition to see how far we could coast down the other side. The record was just shy of two miles, the last few yards gained by everyone getting out of the moving car and heaving furiously to squeeze out the extra yards. This record was set near Piltdown, I recall.

There wasn't much traffic in those days. We could play this game happily all afternoon and see five other cars. Whenever we did encounter a vehicle, its driver, invariably a county fellow, always stopped to offer help to the beautiful redhead in distress. He always looked disappointed when she announced she was OK, pointing out that she already had two perfectly good boys shoving and grunting behind the car.

In the summer Jack brought picnics to Vinehall. She carried a classic wicker basket from Fortnum and Mason's with plates and crockery strapped in, compartments for bottles, a thermos flask, a chilled section for meats and cream cakes. She would pick us up at the usual time—never late—and always gave us a choice: seaside or countryside? I have eternally happy memories of the seaside at Camber, Pevensey, Hastings and Romney Marsh, as of the countryside around Battle, the Weald of Kent and the South Downs. With a bit of effort I could probably define my memory of each beauty spot by the flavour of cream cake I consumed there.

Jack's picnics were a sumptuous departure from the frugal post war food we'd been brought up with. Cold chicken legs and cipolatas, mayonnaise, camembert, baguettes, fresh tomatoes. A baguette, in the 1960's? Yup, Fortnum & Mason's provided everything back then. Still do. Depending on the season, Jack would bring strawberries, raspberries, cherries, a pineapple and other exotica. I ate my first kiwi fruit at one of Jack's picnics. She always brought the most succulent chocolate cakes that would today carry the warning 'death by chocolate'. I don't do chocolate any more but can still taste every mouthful of Jack's cakes, fifty years later.

She once brought a coconut which taxed our ingenuity. Deep in the Sussex countryside, we attempted to open it with the corkscrew of a Swiss army knife, we tried bashing it like Neanderthals with a piece of flint lying in a field. Geoffrey suggested that Jack should drive over it: that would be certain to crack it. We positioned the coconut in front of the rear tyre and signalled Jack to move slowly forward. She revved the engine. The Wolseley slowly mounted it. Suddenly the tyre thumped over the coconut, spinning furiously and, in a shower of gravel, shot it like a cannonball into the woods. We never found it.

We discovered Drusilla's, near Alfriston. It was a quirky tea shop and a petting zoo where we sometimes went after our freewheeling adventures in the Downs. If we'd spent the day in that part of Sussex our Sunday tea would be at Drusilla's rather than the Yew Tree Inn.

Jack sometimes took us for half term, which meant having two young boys to stay for a week in her care at Cavendish Square. If Jack was working during the day, Jill picked up the slack and took time off to entertain us in London. I'm amazed—and grateful -- looking back, how those busy twins made so much time for us.

They took us to Kew and Hampton Court by boat, where I lost myself, and my sense of humour, in the maze. We sailed down river to Greenwich, where we had a cherry pip spitting contest. Alastair won when he gobbed a horizontal distance of 25 feet. We visited Madame Tussaud's and the Natural History Museum, the National Portrait Gallery and the Odeon Leicester Square. Here I saw Hailey Mills in Pollyanna. She transformed my life at the age of 10: I was thunderstruck that such a gorgeous creature might possibly walk on the same planet as me.

I have two memories of Jack administering to me in sickness.

Sports Day 1961 was the occasion in which I was going to prove my athletic prowess over Lingwood, Bruton and Traversi. I had aced the trials and expected to win the three events in which we competed: 100 yard sprint, long jump and high jump. I woke at seven o'clock that bright Whitsun Saturday with a piece of grit in my left eye. I tried to wash it out with cold water but it got worse. My eye was inflamed, really sore. I went to Sister in the san, who prescribed 3 drops from a small brown bottle, and two hours rest.

Sports day didn't officially begin until noon, when parents arrived with their picnics, so there would be plenty of time for the grit to work its way out of my eye. In the meantime, Sister counselled, don't panic and rest up, all would be fine. Well, it wasn't. My eye got progressively worse. Dr Maxwell said I had conjunctivitis. He prescribed a gauze pad soaked in witch hazel, pressed to my eye with a black patch held onto my head with firm elastic. He said I would have to be off games.

Jack arrived at noon with her Fortnum's picnic basket packed with fizzy apple juice (no cider on school grounds), cold cipolatas, croissants, cream cheese, chicken drumsticks, packets of Smiths crisps with little blue wax paper twist containing the salt, Scottish shortbread and, of course, glutinous slabs of chocolate cake.

When I ran up to the Wolseley she laughed when she saw my eye patch. She thought I was playing pirates. But I burst into tears and told her that I had conjunctivitis, was off games and worst of all, I wasn't allowed near the events in case I infected other boys.

I spent Sports Day skulking around the fringes of the athletics field, not talking to anyone, but near enough to hear the taunts of skiving from my competitors. After a tearful picnic, Jack wisely suggested that we should leave the event before the afternoon traffic built up into London.

By the time I'd returned to school after half term I was cured of conjunctivitis but my athletic pedestal was firmly occupied by others. Jack dismissed the whole thing as unimportant and sent a lemon sponge cake to Vinehall for everybody to share.

Then she nursed me at the end of Christmas Term 1962 during a flu epidemic. The school wanted to get the children away home as soon as possible. She drove resolutely to Vinehall, bundled me into her car, filled me with Haliborange and drove back to London. By the time we'd arrived at Cavendish Square I was a wreck. She nursed me for two days until my mother returned from overseas and took me to Scotland by sleeper from Kings Cross. Whenever I take Haliborange or Vitamin C supplements today, I think of Jack.

Our prep-school jaunts ended six months before they should have. I still feel embarrassed by my carelessness in taking Jack for granted. It was always understood that she would be at Vinehall at 11 o'clock every third Sunday, after church. No specific plans had to be made; there was standing permission from the school, the arrangement was permanent and reliable. One October Sunday she wasn't there at 11 o'clock. She hadn't shown up by half-past. Geoffrey and I hung around the school steps, wondering. There was no phone call or message. Maybe she'd forgotten? Maybe she'd got the date wrong? Maybe we'd got the day wrong.

Just before noon, a local Robertsbridge mother arrived to

collect her son. She saw two disconsolate boys on the school steps and asked if we'd like to come out for lunch. We explained the situation. She left a note at the school office to say that if Jack showed up she should come to Robertsbridge and pick us up.

Not long after we'd driven off, Jack and Jill did show up at the school. They followed instructions and arrived at my friend's door just as we were sitting down for lunch. It was clear that we were well-ensconced and enjoying ourselves. Very thoughtfully Jack offered us a choice; we could stay with our friends, or, if our hostess didn't mind, come with her and have the usual Jack picnic in the country somewhere.

Our hostess made it absolutely clear that it was OK for us to go off with my aunts, but the Robertsbridge option just seemed more exciting. Our friend had an airgun, and we were going to do some target practice on a line of tin cans after lunch. We declined Jack's offer. She hugged me, easing my embarrassment by saying she wouldn't want to go out with her old auntie either. I felt a twinge of guilt as the car chugged off down the lane. She never came to Vinehall again.

MIDDLE YEARS

There was one final jaunt, in fact. Two years later I was at school in the Far North. Jack was coming to Aberdeen for a dental conference, and offered to take Alastair and me out for lunch the following Sunday. We accepted with alacrity, as families rarely ventured that far to take their boys out. It turned out that the Queen was visiting the area that Sunday and Jack was held up by heavy security, but we eventually escaped for a boozy lunch at the Gordon Arms in Fochabers.

Jack had begun to treat me as a young man; for my part I had started to sense that she was quite a big cheese in her professional world. As we parted on that occasion, she declared that we would always be welcome to stay in London, and that we "could show up in Cavendish Square any time at all."

The following July I responded to this offer rather too literally. 1967 was the Summer of Love (so-called: I didn't get any, did you?) Foolish young fellows were packing bags and sticking their thumbs out on roadsides all over Europe and North America. Kids were on the move. The Age of Aquarius was long before the Age of Ipod, but we somehow managed to groove along to Whiter Shade of Pale, San Francisco, Waterloo Sunset, On the Road Again and, of course, All You Need is Love. Every juke box in the Western world played those songs incessantly that summer, though I never did figure out why the lights went out in Massachusetts.

Hitch hiking was the normal way to get around. Parents

seemed remarkably relaxed about their teenagers travelling rough around the world. Or maybe they weren't relaxed, but realized that their disapproval would make no difference. Or maybe, as in my case, they simply didn't know.

The mood was happy that Friday morning in July as I took a bus to the southernmost stop in Edinburgh. The sun was shining. I walked three hundred yards to a spot where vehicles could pull off the A1, and stuck out my thumb. My first ride, five minutes later, took me to Newcastle. I was in York by lunchtime and Peterborough by five. I was deposited on Watford High Street at eight-thirty. I thought it might be a good idea to phone Jack at this point. The call went something like this:

"Oh, hello. It's me. How are you?"

"Very well, thank you." came the cagey response.

"Er, well, I was wondering what you..."

"Where are you?"

"I'm on Watford High Street."

"Where are you staying in London?"

"Er...I'm not sure yet."

"Well, you'd better come over." she said firmly, but I could hear a groan in her voice. She added, "Try to come as quickly as you can because I'm going out to dinner. Take the tube from Watford High Street to Oxford Circus. Cavendish Square's just around the corner."

"Brilliant."

I hadn't connected the convertible silver Bentley Continental parked on the double yellows with Jack. As I approached the steps to 19 Harcourt House, she shouted from the passenger seat:

"Look Gavin, I don't have anything to eat in the house. You'd better come with us."

I saw the look of well-bred disappointment—you might call it a sneer—in the face of her escort. He was a highly-eligible, super-hip peer of the realm. I recognised him from the top-tier glamour mags that lay around the senior common room at school. He was famous for his cars and conquests of beautiful women. He was said to groove in Cannes and with the Rolling Stones crowd. Now Jack was inviting me to interrupt what might have been the night of her life.

I was filthy from fourteen hours of hitch hiking and smelled like a polecat. I was tired, dirty and unkempt. Yet graciously, our stud gestured to the back seat, "Hop in, old man. I hope you like French cooking."

A glamorous dinner had been set for two at the best French restaurant in Chelsea. The *maître d'* didn't bat an eyelid when he was commanded to add another setting. Milord was chatty and personable. He knew many of the parents of my school friends. He rested his hand on Jack's knee, which she did nothing to encourage. About midnight he drove us home. He didn't come upstairs; I crashed out.

Reflecting on that evening over the years, I've had many residual thoughts. First, maybe it was cooler than I realised for Milord to be seen with what might pass as a real hippie in London in the summer of 1967. I was so knackered that I probably appeared unimpressed by his trappings of status. Second, Jack was extraordinarily loyal and kind to have compromised a date with one of the most eligible men in the land. For me. BUT, is it possible that I saved her from a fate worse than death? He was a well-known cad. Who knows?

When I was about to leave her flat to hitchhike to France a few days later, Jack gave me one simple ground rule for the future: one week's notice, please, before turning up. That was all she said on the subject.

My life raced off at that point: university, girlfriends, multiple preoccupations, starting a career in law, then finance. Jack and I were always punctilious about Christmas cards and birthdays, and shared occasional meals together, but London was not my beat, so we drifted apart until much later in life.

LATER JAUNTS

I'd watched my mother's lights dim painfully over several years and witnessed her death as the last bulb fizzled out. Although she had occasionally made self-aware comments like "Lord, how I miss my mind", Dr Alzheimer had blanked her brain. My mother was well cared-for in extreme old age, but I've never believed that my feelings for her got through. I have a list of regrets I wish I could have discussed and, one by one, received her forgiveness. But it didn't happen.

When my mother died I was determined to leave no stone unturned with Jack. For a start, there was no baggage: she was my aunt, after all. We spun no complicated web of unfulfilled wishes, harsh words, guilt or unspoken regrets. Quite simply, as I saw her becoming more frail and vulnerable, it seemed right to give her as much time in old age as she had given me as a child. Her special friend, Alan, had died in the summer of 2008; she was finding it harder to cope. We made a family decision that she should move to Scotland.

In November 2009 I rented a white Ford Transit van from Arnold Clark in Dundee and headed South on the A1. Eight hours later I reached Steeple Bumpstead. Jack had already decided what furniture she wanted. She had sorted her clothes, books, linens, crockery, tools, papers, wicker baskets and all the accumulated mementoes of a well-lived life. She had donated piles of things to charity shops, divided her art between friends and given away objects to people who'd admired them over the years. She was generous and matter-of-fact: "Everything should belong to the person who loves it most, you know".

In the morning I packed Jack's remaining effects into the Ford Transit. I watched her moving slowly around the cottage, bidding a silent farewell to each room. At nine o'clock she closed the front door and gave me the keys. I helped her into the passenger seat and reversed into Church Street for the last time. Dear, sweet Ron, her ever-watchful neighbour, stood on his top step waving dejectedly, whippet at his feet. It was raining lightly. Jack never looked back.

Jack was like a kid as we drove north. She had never sat so high in a vehicle: the Ford Transit put us above other cars on the road. She could see over the hedgerows, the views were different from those she was familiar with. She would exclaim 'I never knew there was a country house over there.' Or, 'That car's got a dirty roof'.

We stopped for a late lunch at the Scotch Corner Hotel where we worked our way through sizeable steak pies; Jack enjoyed a glass of red wine. A woman came up to us in the dining area and asked, "Are you Miss Ritchie?"

"Yes. Who are you?"

"I've worked at this hotel for years. I remember you as a regular here."

Jack had always made a point of stopping at the Scotch Corner Hotel on her way north, from the 1950s to the last time she'd driven to Scotland with Alan in 2006. Then she always stopped on the way south again.

"That's very reassuring." she replied. And it was.

You generally don't expect to see a distinguished elderly lady in the passenger seat of a white Ford Transit van. She received dozens of double-takes as we overtook trucks, vans and cars in the fast lane heading north. Jack grinned at astonished truckers, plasterer's mates, back-seat kids and travelling salesmen, waving cheerily from her Ford Transit throne as we zoomed past.

We reached our destination at dusk. The Scottish weather was damper and rougher than Steeple Bumpstead's had been that morning, 500 miles south. Terrill, my wife, had worked hard to ensure that the cottage was warm and welcoming for Jack's arrival. We helped her out of the van and escorted her through the front door. I was reminded of a TV documentary about re-housing a gorilla. The creature very tentatively surveys his new space, slowly traces the fence that defines his territory, pats a tree trunk, pushes the swing gingerly, looks at but doesn't touch his food tray. Then with a grunt of approval, he jumps onto the tree trunk and starts munching a piece of fruit.

So with Jack. Even though she had been fully involved at every stage of the cottage's restoration and knew exactly what to expect, she looked carefully around the rooms without a word. Finally Terrill looked at me quizzically and spoke:

"Welcome to your new home."

Jack replied, “Not until I’ve had a whisky.”

Out came The Macallan and she never looked back.

Within 48 hours everything was deployed exactly how Jack wanted it. As she settled in we immediately involved her in our daily lives. She joined us for family meals, she came shopping, we took her to events she might find interesting; we visited her every day with dogs and children. She enjoyed the attention and family warmth, but soon commented that she’d always been independent. She was very happy to read her Daily Telegraph in the morning and snooze in the afternoon. She preferred to have meals earlier than us; she liked to get up –and go to bed– very early. She was finding our pace a bit frenetic.

We evolved to a more independent approach. Jack wasn’t able to prepare her own meals, so we engaged a local service called Abbey Care to cook her lunch five times a week. They came to her cottage and cooked from ingredients she had selected, which meant that she ate more or less what she would have cooked for herself.

We registered Jack with the Kirriemuir Health Centre; she was allocated a care worker whose name was Marie. Marie made it a priority to get to know Jack, then kept in touch at regular intervals to ensure that she was provided optimal service. She understood the deadening march of Alzheimer’s and our many thanks go to her for helping plan Jack’s old age care so successfully.

What about the other two days of the week? I gave Jack a list of places within an hour's drive and told her to choose where she wanted to have lunch. She came up with the classic Jack response:

"I want to try every one of these places."

"Which would you like to go to today?"

She stuck her finger on the list at random. It landed on the Park Tavern at Drumshademuir, a restaurant on the road just north of Glamis.

"Here." she said firmly.

"Excellent. That's where we'll go today." I helped with her coat, she brandished her stick with a flourish and we tottered to the car.

Not five minutes later, we drew up at our destination.

The Park Tavern is owned by Jim Duncan. It is situated beside a caravan park and has a reputation for tasty, hot, well-priced food. It has a varied menu, prices are reasonable and crucially from Jack's point of view, they serve a big glass of red wine. Over the next two years the Park Tavern became a regular haunt. As soon as the car pulled up outside, our table was ready. Jack's back was always against the radiator, the glass of red wine in place before she took her seat. I stuck to ginger beer.

We rarely needed to go further than the *menu du jour* on a fixed price. On the first day our meal consisted of breast of chicken, skirlie, Bretagne leek sauce and chips. (Boiled tatties are always available for health nuts).

As I escorted Jack down the exit ramp she couldn't resist a bit of cheeky banter with two old chaps sitting at the bar.

"Top marks." she remarked as we left the Park Tavern, "We'll be back."

In the following weeks we drove further afield. Jack could still walk but was increasingly immobile. She loved being driven around, inhaling the glens, the lochs, sheep and cattle. One such destination was Glen Clova. By the time we'd reached the hotel the rain was sweeping up the valley in dense grey curtains. The disabled parking was reasonably close, but Jack wasn't dressed warmly enough to make it to the hotel without getting soaked.

"Hang on, I've got an idea." I left the motor running to keep her warm and ran across the drenched car park into the lobby. A young man was serving behind the bar.

"Can I help you?"

"Well, I have an unusual request. My elderly aunt is sitting in the car outside. She can't make it inside. Is there any chance I could take food out to the car for her?"

"Aye—nae sweat. What would ye like?" The young man

sounded as if this was the most exciting thing to happen so far that day.

I perused the menu, ordering two cups of Cullen Skink accompanied by stilton & walnut toasties. I ordered the usual red wine for Jack and ginger beer for me. I paid the bill and picked up a copy of the Press & Journal while I waited.

"Ye don't haftae wait, I'll bring it oot when it's ready."

"Sure? It's absolutely pouring out there today."

"It's absolutely pouring out there every day." he replied laconically.

Ten minutes later a shrouded figure carrying a covered tray tapped on the car window. I wound it down and the young man handed us the tray in a lashing flurry of raindrops.

"I'll be back in a while with the empties." I told him.

There was a vast sense of *déjà vu* as Jack and I sipped soup and munched our sandwiches in the car, rain pounding on the steamed-up windows. World at One was on the radio; I rejoiced at the circularity of it all.

"Remember those outings from Vinehall fifty years ago in the Sussex Downs? Remember Camber Sands?"

"Of course," she laughed. "I just have trouble remembering what I did this morning."

The young man seemed surprised to be tipped for his efforts when I returned with the tray half an hour later. We continued our drive to the top of the glen, where we finally turned into the teeth of the gale for the road home. We didn't pass a single vehicle all the way back.

Jack decided she wanted to go shopping in Perth. She needed to go to Marks & Spencer and suggested lunch afterwards. It was an opportunity to explore new territory. Many people had spoken highly of the Gloagburn Farm Shop in Tibbermore, so after Jack had stocked up with her smalls at M&S we dumped them in the car boot and drove west.

It was one o'clock on a weekday. Gloagburn was packed. After a long wait we were eventually shown a seat through a throng of tables and given a menu. I'd been worried about Jack's stamina for standing in a queue but once we'd sat down her mood improved. She worked her way through a fish plate; my chicken and mushroom pastie was excellent. The place was crowded with mothers and young families but Jack loved an audience. She inspected the mouth of one small girl who ventured too close to our table and pronounced that she had Very Good Teeth, to the child's surprise and her mother's pride.

If there was time after lunch I often took her for a drive into the hills. I'd bundle her into the front passenger seat and head somewhere like Dunkeld, Pitlochry or Braemar. If she was up to it, we'd stop for tea. However much she'd eaten for lunch she always had space for a pot of Earl Grey and a slice of home-baked cake. Distant echoes of the Yew Tree. It was my duty to feed her as much as possible; she was a thin old lady just as she'd been a willowy young woman.

As we drove through some of the most soul-inspiring scenery on the planet, we would often have conversations like this:

"This reminds me of Scotland." observed Jack

"Well, yes."

"I wonder who planted those trees?"

"The Forestry Commission, perhaps?"

"Who?"

"The Forestry Commission."

"The Forestry Commission?"

"Yes. They commission forests."

She found this hilariously funny for some reason.

Then after five minutes,

"This reminds me of Scotland."

And so forth. She always returned to her opening observation, which made our conversations pleasantly circular, a bit like the old song, “There’s a hole in my bucket … “

The progress of Jack’s Dementia has not been linear. On some days she’s on the ball, interested, well-informed and outgoing; on others she makes no sense at all. But intriguingly she always seems to make sense to herself; she doesn’t seem aware that her words have come out garbled. A perfectly rational observation like “Those sheep must be very cold on the hill.” might come out as, “They should really knock down the lamp post”, to which I’ll respond, “Yes, they should really knock down the lamp post”. She then looks at me oddly and obviously thinks I’m nuts.

I would sometimes knock on the door of her cottage after lunch and find her napping in her chair, the Daily Telegraph open on her lap. In a stage whisper, I’d say, “Oh well, never mind, I was thinking of driving to Peel Farm.” To which one eye would open and she’d answer, “I trust you’re not thinking of going without me.”

There ensued the usual palaver of dressing her up and bundling her into the front seat of the car. She emulated her own mother—my grandmother—who always said, “Bottoms first, Mrs R.” whenever she boarded a car. So Jack always braced herself by saying, “Bottoms first, Miss R.” before sliding into the passenger seat.

There are several ways to Peel Farm from Jack’s cottage. You must start by driving north around Kirriemuir and past Kinnordy Loch, then you can choose the direct route or the meandering route. The direct route takes you through sheep-filled pastureland in the midst of the serene panorama of Lintrathan Loch and its surrounding woodland. The meandering route takes you deeper into the hills as far as Balintore, one of the most atmospheric castles in Scotland. The castle glowers at the head of a glen, visible for a great distance. As you approach the building you realise that it's ruined. The castle has been pillaged over the years and quarried for its fine stones. Lintels and embrasures have been ripped out, slates stolen from the roof, staircases levered out of the building, floorboards, doors, cupboards stolen.

The spirit of Balintore is of neglect and dereliction. It's hard to imagine that the castle was ever loved, though Jack was attracted by the romance of the place, its grandeur; she loved the jackdaws nesting in the turrets. I always drove past slowly for her to enjoy the view before heading off to Peel Farm. Recently a gentleman has bought the castle and plans to restore it slate by slate, timber by timber, stone by stone, God bless him.

Peel Farm has two shops: one sells smart accessories, the other sells plants, meat and old china. Then there's The Tea Room. I can't remember who said, "If you build it, they will come." but it rings true in the context of rural Scotland. Here, you can create a Tea Room around any farmyard or disused silage pit and with a bit of effort it will do well. There's something about the dank rawness of a Scottish day, any day, frankly, that makes a person yearn for low ceilings, a good fug, a crowded room, a pot of strong tea and a cream cake. The more remote the location, the more it beckons.

The first sight that greets you on entering the Tea Room is the display cabinet stacked with creamy sponge cakes. I must have taken Jack there ten times—sometimes for lunch, more often for tea. She always demolishes a large slab of cake with her teaspoon, then exclaims, "And you know I don't really like cake." After tea she enjoys looking around the shops and watching the geese and ducks in the farmyard. Nearby there's a spectacular walk along a river gorge called Reekie Lynn, which is a great place to work off a heavy tea. But I have to leave Jack in the car facing the view. The walk is far too arduous for her.

The Tea-shop was once so crowded that we were turned away. We skipped lunch there and drove to Alyth instead. The Lands of Loyal is a Victorian country house hotel with a splendid armorial staircase and panelled corridors. Some of the fittings in the hall came from the Mauretania, which gives guests a fine sense of occasion. With a full glass of red wine before her Jack settled into lamb cutlets and a salad, declaring herself very pleased with life.

Our trips into the countryside were always unplanned. We'd set off in the late morning in a new direction, with the vague idea of a destination, and see what fortune delivered. These trips were often eventful, or seemed to have consequences beyond coincidence. For instance I thought Jack might like to see St Cyrus again, given that she'd long spoken of her childhood holidays and even expressed the wish to have her ashes spread there "If I ever get round to dying".

So one morning we set out towards Stonehaven. It was a

lovely September day with light clouds scudding overhead. When we reached St Cyrus we drove along to the cliff-top car park. It faced east towards a huge vista of sky, sea and sand vanishing into a pink mist of sea spray. Jack was happy to take in the view from the car as I belted down the cliff pathway to see where the family campsite had been located in the 1920s. I'm not certain if Jack had pointed out the right location, but it doesn't really matter, does it? St Cyrus is a concept, a distant paradise that lives in the heart of an old lady. After reporting back that the campsite was still pristine I took her to lunch in the coffee shop we'd passed earlier.

The Old Bakery Coffee Shop was on the corner of the main road and the side road leading to the beach. We were served steaming bowls of soup, sandwiches and, later, coffee and cakes. Jack insisted to the waitress, "I remember this place. I used to come here when I was a young girl." It was unlikely that this coffee shop had been there eighty years earlier, but it's possible that an Old Bakery had been on the site, and that Jack and Jill had been sent up the hill, so to speak, to fetch the morning bread. The young waitress replied politely, "That's very interesting."

One thing is for certain. Jack may or may not have had a past connection with the Old Bakery Coffee Shop, but she unquestionably has no future there. A few days after our visit in September 2010, a car smashed into the Coffee Shop and damaged it so severely that it had to be closed. When I read her the article from the Courier, she muttered, "Dangerous places, those tea rooms."

Our jaunts did not always revolve around teacakes and lunch. Jack had been a lifelong member of the National Trust for Scotland and wanted to visit The House of Dun. We picked a fine Spring day and headed towards Montrose. We began our visit with (surprise, surprise) a coffee and cake at the café, chatting to the amiable lady with a Texas accent who managed the place.

We enjoyed visiting the house and learning about its history, the gardens were beautifully manicured, but on our way out Jack stopped in the courtyard. She announced, "Time's wrong."

"What do you mean?"

"Time's wrong. Look!"

Sure enough the courtyard clock's two faces were both stuck at nine thirty. It was one thirty.

"I'll borrow a ladder and wind it up." I suggested helpfully.

"No, it's broken." Jack replied authoritatively, "It needs to be fixed."

She'd always been a bit of a clock aficionado and Knew About These Things.

"Well that's that, then."

"No, I'll pay to have it repaired."

This was very typical of Jack's generosity. If she could make the world a better place on a snap decision, she would. After making enquiries we established that the clock at The House of Dun was on a list of items to be repaired, so Jack contributed the required sum to the NTS. As I write eighteen months later the clock remains stuck at nine thirty, but I'm assured that the matter is in hand.

There are dozens of hostelries I could mention in passing. This is not a travel guide, but I've inserted a list of places that we visited, in an appendix at the back. I haven't rated them beyond anything I've said in this text. One thing is absolutely clear: from the cosiest tea shop to the grandest hotel, all the establishments we visited are managed heart and soul by their owners. It would be extremely unfair to pass judgement on a flaccid chip, a dry bun or a lukewarm coffee when the proprietor works sixteen hours a day to run a business to provide for his family.

It's sad to see a restaurant going out of business. We had a congenial meal last year at the Angler's Inn in Guildtown. The fish was fresh, the salad crisp, the wine was sweet, the service quick, the restaurant animated and warm, the price reasonable. A few weeks later the business closed. It didn't deserve to: behind every closure is a tale of enterprising people who've taken a risk, worked hard and followed their dreams, God bless them.

Those of us who live in Angus or Perthshire are extremely lucky to have such a variety of hostelries to choose from. Never take them for granted, use them often and tell your friends.

They're wonderful places to take your elderly aunt. Besides, they must be kept open for the day my generation is wheeled around the glens by our adventurous descendants.

After two years at the cottage Jack was becoming frail and absent-minded. It was a gentle slope, but viewed over two years, we could see the difference. As a precaution we installed a Community Alarm in her cottage. This meant that she wore a beeper on her wrist like a watch, so if she got into trouble she could press it. The signal would be picked up by a twenty four hour service whose first response would be to call me. If there was no answer from me they would send someone down in a car. The maximum time Jack would be alone in a crisis would be about fifteen minutes.

It didn't take long. At one thirty the next morning our phone rang. A Community Alarm operator had picked up Jack's signal, and would I please investigate? The wind was howling outside; the night was pitch black; rain slashed across the windows. I left our warm bed, heaved a thick coat over my pyjamas, donned a hat and wellies and stumbled across the farm to Jack's cottage. It was unlit. I pushed open the front door, announcing, "Hello Jack, it's me, don't worry."

I turned on the lights. Everything seemed all right. Jack lay in bed, wide awake with a grin on her face. "Not bad at all." She said, "I wondered how long it would take someone to arrive."

"Well, it's important that you know the system works, so I'm glad you tried it out." I tried to sound reasonable but couldn't resist adding, "Just remember the boy who cried Wolf!" I beeped the Operator and told her it had been a false alarm.

A few nights later we were jarred awake by the phone at two fifteen. I rushed through the drill and was at Jack's cottage in nine minutes. Her bedroom light was on, though at first I didn't see her. "Jack? Are you there?"

"I'm here." Came the muffled response. Then I spotted the two spindly legs sticking out from under the bed.

"Are you all right?"

"I think so."

"Are you in any pain? Have you broken anything?"

"No, I don't think so."

"Well, this is a silly place to spend the night." I couldn't figure out how she'd got under the bed and into that position on the floor.

She laughed. She always saw the absurd side of everything.

"Well, I'm going to pull you out slowly. Take this blanket so I don't expose your modesty as you come out".

"You never know, if my night-dress rides up you might get the sight of a lifetime."

"Hmm."

I covered her with the tartan rug, took a firm grip of her ankles and pulled her out like a drawer. She slid into the room with a bemused look on her face.

"Here, let me help you back into bed." After tucking her firmly back between the sheets I beeped the Operator to say it was a false alarm. I never did find out exactly what had happened that night.

Jack believes strongly in charitable giving. Dollar Academy has always been close to her heart. She and her four sisters had been happy and successful at the school, and she wanted to commemorate them somehow. She donated a silver cup and the prize money to institute The Ritchie Prize for Excellence in Science. Every Ritchie girl's name was inscribed on the cup, which has become a coveted science award for sixth-form pupils at the school.

Each year the Academy invites her to the Summer Prize Giving ceremony. The last time she attended was in 2011. She was eighty eight and frail, but still able to walk—just. I stopped the car in front of the pillared entrance of the school. Without prompting, two teenage girls opened the passenger door and helped her out. They walked her up the steps and into the building. By the time I'd parked the car and caught up with her she was surrounded by pupils and staff, telling them "On the best authority," that she was "the oldest surviving head girl of Dollar Academy." They loved this feisty old lady and mobbed her like a celebrity.

We were given seats in the back row of the auditorium with a good view of the podium. As soon as we sat down Jack turned to me and said "I feel like I've come home." I put my arm around her shoulder. The crowd hushed when the Rector stood up and began, in a portentous tone,

"Before we commence the proceedings today, I have an important announcement to make. We are privileged today to have in our midst a very distinguished guest..."

People looked around. Nelson Mandela? Bill Clinton? Shirley Bassey?

"Someone who has had a very long association with Dollar Academy."

More expectant looks.

"I would like to accord a very warm welcome to Miss Joan Ritchie, the Head Girl of Dollar Academy in 1940."

The crowd broke out in warm applause and many kids, particularly girls, cheered loudly. When the applause died down a little voice rang out from the back, "Was that me he was talking about?"

BALHOUSIE

In October 2011 I went on a hiking trip in the Pyrenees. The family kept an eye on Jack, routinely popping in to see her. This was in addition to Abbey Care at lunchtime and a Community service in the evenings. On the morning before I returned, Jack fell in the bathroom. She fell in a position that somehow prevented her from reaching her Community Alarm button. She'd lain in considerable discomfort and confusion for several hours, we believe, before she was discovered and the alarm was raised.

The medical services jumped into action. Her doctor from Kirriemuir arrived immediately: Jack was in shock and needed medical care. An ambulance was called. Within the hour Jack was in Dundee's Ninewells Hospital under observation. She was confused and uncoordinated but fundamentally well: there was no breakage, infection or obvious ailment. After a few days it was clear that she didn't need to be in a healing ward in hospital. The problem was psychological but real at the same time: Jack could no longer walk.

She was cheerful and agreed to two weeks' convalescence at Whitehills in Forfar. Marie helped with this placement. The idea was that she should be under observation, receive intensive physiotherapy on her legs and return home, hopefully, to resume her previous life. Whitehills is a spanking new facility with a focus on convalescence, minor drop-ins and palliative care. It represents the very best of the NHS: clean, well-designed, efficient and staffed by people who obviously enjoy being there.

A lady physiotherapist was assigned to Jack. Her task was to investigate the cause of the problem and get Jack on her feet again. The physio worked hard to help her to walk but met complete resistance. She found no physical symptoms. It was unclear whether the disability had been triggered by her fall or by a quirk of Dementia whereby signals from her brain were no longer received by her legs. She was afraid to stand and would need help with most physical functions for the rest of her life. I tried to explain this, but Jack cheerfully replied that she'd get by just fine. She had not given up; she'd simply accepted her new condition entirely without self-pity.

In the search for twenty four hour care, Marie helped us understand what to look for in a nursing home for Jack. I spent a week wandering about Tayside inspecting geriatric homes from the coast of Angus to the hills of Perthshire. I met many dedicated managers who clearly loved their jobs. They walked me around their premises, showed me the room which Jack would be given and let me chat to long-term residents.

My early preference was for a Scottish baronial pile converted into a nursing home with a wonderful view of the hills. The staff had a nice sense of humour, the place was atmospheric and the residents had been well-travelled. Many sipped glasses of sherry before meals and enjoyed a whisky last thing at night. I thought, "Hmm. Not a bad place to spend one's declining years. Not bad at all."

Terrill thought otherwise. She argued in favour of an advanced-technology custom-built home in Coupar Angus run by the Balhousie Care Group, which is just as well: I had nearly sent Jack back to my prep school.

Jack's move to Coupar Angus seemed terribly final. We'd all accepted the reality that she'd never live independently again. She would need help for all movement, she would never prepare a meal again, bathe, dress herself, see the world ...

Most days I make the forty mile round-trip to catch up with her. Every time I ask how she is, she replies, "I'm content." She must have known in her heart when she came north that her stay in the farm cottage would be brief and that she would end up in a nursing home. My vision had always been to keep her going as long as possible, independent and in her own place. But reflecting on matters since she's been installed at Balhousie, her current situation seems right. Jack is peaceful and content with her lot.

POSTSCRIPT

Jack died on December 17th 2012. It had been a gradual and seemingly painless slide. She recognized visitors and managed a chuckle right to the end. In the weeks before she died, two amusing incidents were reported to me by the staff at Balhousie. One morning the nurses entered her room to get her up, wash and feed her. It was one of those days when she simply did not want to move, so she pulled a sheet over her head and in a muffled voice, announced, "I'm not in today." A few nights later one of the nurses was on her rounds and looked in on Jack. She was lying on her back, absolutely still. The worried nurse turned her ear to Jack's mouth to listen for breath, when Jack opened one eye and exclaimed, "Ha! Fooled you!"

Terrill and I spent much of Jack's last day at her bedside. The doctor had given her a morphine shot to mitigate the pain of her bedsores; Handel's Messiah was playing on the radio. As her breath became more laboured, she looked at us in turn and said quietly, "I think I'll go upstairs now." Thus Jack slipped away. We were reassured by her confidence that she was heading upstairs rather than downstairs, and I'm sure she's in a good place now.

In many places the text of this book was written in the present tense. I see no reason to change it to the past tense. Jack was a great personality and remains a large presence in the lives of those who knew her.

APPENDIX

A list of hostelries frequented in Jack's jaunts:

The Angler's Inn, Guildtown
Ballathie House Hotel, Meiklour
Bein Inn, Glenfarg
Belmont Arms, Meigle
Bridges, Kirriemuir
But & Ben, Auchmithie
Castle Hotel, Newtyle
Drovers, Memus
Glen Clova Hotel, Clova
Gloagburn Farm, Tibbermore
Gordon's Restaurant, Inverkeillor
Green Hotel, Kinross
House of Dun, Montrose
Kinloch House Hotel, Blairgowrie
Kookaburra, Auchterforfar
Lands of Loyal, Alyth
Links Hotel, Montrose
MacDonald Arms Hotel, Balbeggie
Meiklour Hotel, Meiklour
Murton Farm, Forfar
Old Bakery, St Cyrus
Old Brewhouse, Arbroath
Park Tavern, Drumshademuir
Peel Farm, Isla
Ramsay Arms, Fettercairn
Red House Hotel, Coupar Angus
The Swan, Brechin

The Swan, Kirriemuir
Scottish Antique Centre, Abernyte
Strathmore Arms, Glamis
Tormaukin, Glendevon
Trumperton Forge